Copyright © 2003 by Nord-Süd Verlag AG, Gossau Zürich, Switzerland
First published in Switzerland under the title *Pirat Wirbelwind zieht um*.
English translation copyright © 2003 by North-South Books Inc., New York

First published in the United States, Great Britain, Canada, Australia,
and New Zealand in 2003 by North-South Books, an imprint
of Nord-Süd Verlag AG, Gossau Zürich, Switzerland.

Distributed in the United States by North-South Books Inc., New York.

Library of Congress Cataloging-in-Publication Data is available.
A CIP catalogue record for this book is available from The British Library.
ISBN 0-7358-1832-0 (trade edition)
1 3 5 7 9 HC 10 8 6 4 2
ISBN 0-7358-1833-9 (library edition)
1 3 5 7 9 LE 10 8 6 4 2

Printed in Switzerland

For more information about our books, and the authors and artists
who create them, visit our web site: www.northsouth.com

PIRATE PETE SETS SAIL

By Jean-Pierre Jäggi
Illustrated by Alan Clarke

Translated by J. Alison James

NORTH-SOUTH BOOKS

New York / London

PiRATE PETE and his trusty
mates were setting sail for a
new island.

Their treasure had grown too large to fit in the old hideout. At first, Pirate Pete didn't want to move, but a journey on the high seas was always an adventure.

Before they set out, they had to pack.
Pirate Pete took charge of stowing his
hammock, his pirate flag, and his parrot,
Sam.

The mates loaded the ship's dark hold. It was hard work. Pirate Pete kept a list and made sure that nothing was forgotten.

Anchors away! Hoist the mainsail!
Unfurl the jib! The ship moved off.
Pirate Pete waved good-bye to his friends.
He would miss them, but he promised to
send messages in bottles.

It was smooth sailing until a huge galleon blocked their path. The first mate sounded the charge, but the enemy slowly sailed off without returning fire.

In a port far from home, the pirates loaded up with fresh provisions for the rest of the journey. Holy halibut, it was a great place!

"Land ho!" cried Pirate Pete, spotting
the new island from the crow's nest.
"Come about! Hard to port! Mind the yardarm!
Loose the halyard! Lower the boom!
Trim the sails! **DON'T CRASH INTO THE CLIFFS!**"

Pirate Pete dropped anchor, furled the sails, and jumped ashore. While his mates were busy unloading supplies, he unlocked their new hideout.

Pirate Pete set off to explore.
The hideout was large and full
of dark caves for stashing treasure.

Suddenly he spied a native. She was wearing a golden crown and leading a lion on a leash. She must be the daughter of a chief, Pirate Pete decided.

Sure enough, she was Firewire, the Pirate Queen! She showed Pirate Pete her treasure trove. That was it! Pirate Pete knew that this was the perfect place for him.